WRITTEN BY BECCA WRIGHT
EDITED BY LARA MURPHY
DESIGNED BY DERRIAN BRADDER
COVER DESIGN BY ANGIE ALLISON

• • • • • • • • • • • • • • • • •

♥ WITH SPECIAL THANKS TO FRANCES EVANS ♥

Published in Great Britain in 2022 by Buster Books, an imprint of
Michael O'Mara Books Limited, 9 Lion Yard, Tremadoc Road, London SW4 7NQ

 www.mombooks.com/buster   Buster Books   @BusterBooks   @buster_books

A CIP catalogue record for this book is available from the British Library.

ISBN: 978-1-78055-831-8

PLEASE NOTE: This book is not affiliated with or endorsed by BTS,
HYBE/Big Hit Entertainment or any of their publishers or licensees.

1 3 5 7 9 10 8 6 4 2

This book was printed in July 2022 by
Shenzhen Wing King Tong Paper Products Co. Ltd.,
Shenzhen, Guangdong, China.

Picture credits

Front cover: Steve Granitz/WireImage/Getty Images
Back cover: Astrid Stawiarz/Stringer/Getty Images

Page 2–3: Kevin Winter/Getty Images; Page 6–7: The Chosunilbo JNS/Getty Images; Page 8: ilgan
Sports/Getty Images; Page 9: Han Myung-Gu/Getty Images; Page 11: Jeff Kravitz/Getty Images;
Page 13: The Chosunilbo JNS/Getty Images; Page 14: Chelsea Guglielmino/Getty Images; Page 15:
Everett Collection Inc/Alamy Stock Photo; Page 17: Sara Jaye Weiss/Shutterstock; Page 19:
The Chosunilbo JNS/Getty Images; Page 21: Han Myung-Gu/Getty Images; Page 25: THE FACT/
Getty Images; Page 27: The Chosunilbo JNS/Getty Images; Page 28–29: MediaPunch Inc/Alamy
Stock Photo; Page 31: Frazer Harrison/Getty Images; Page 33: Jeff Kravitz/Getty Images; Page 39:
The Chosunilbo JNS/Getty Images; Page 41: JTBC PLUS/Getty Images; Page 47: JNI/Star Max/
Getty Images; Page 49: THE FACT/Getty Images; Page 51: AMA2020/Getty Images; Page 53:
JTBC PLUS/Getty Images; Page 55: Steven Ferdman/Stringer/Getty Images; Page 61:
Matt Winkelmeyer/Getty Images; Page 62–63: Jeff Kravitz/Getty Images

BTS

TOP OF K-POP

Buster Books

CONTENTS

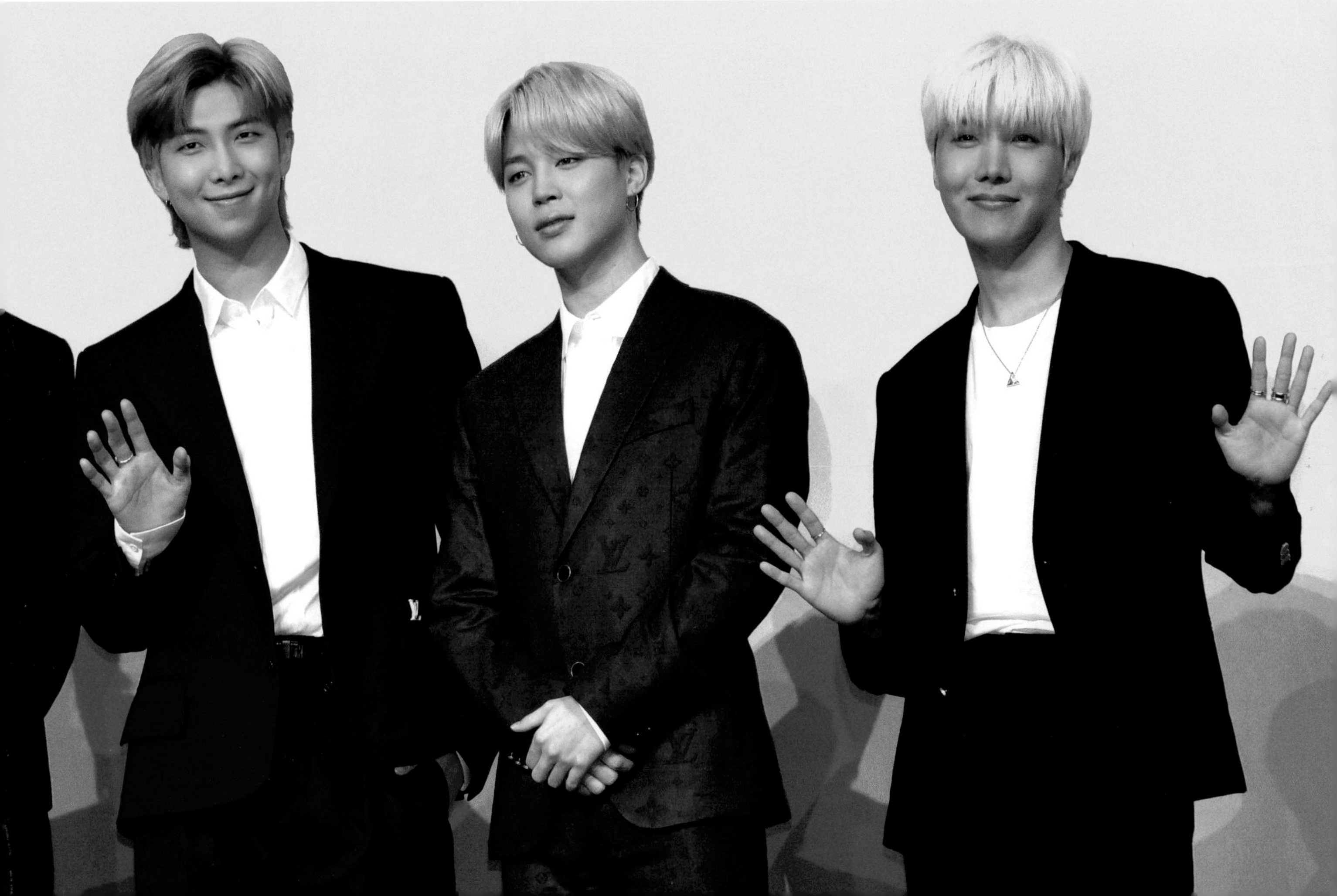

BTS BEGINS (2013-2017)

>>>>

It all began with Bang Si-hyuk (aka Hitman Bang). Way back in 2005, Bang Si-hyuk was working for JYP Entertainment, writing and producing hit songs. After a string of successes, he decided that he wanted to start his own company and founded Big Hit Entertainment. By 2010, he was scouting for members to form a new hip-hop idol group – the group that would become BTS.

Kim Namjoon, aka RM, was the first to be recruited, having made a name for himself as a talented rapper. Shortly after, a promising young rapper/producer named Min Yoongi, aka Suga, joined RM in the Big Hit dorms. He was followed by an award-winning street dancer, Jung Hoseok, aka J-Hope, who had to learn from the others how to rap, as he'd never done it before.

TAKING SHAPE

As the group started to take shape, Bang Si-hyuk decided to change direction: a group of idol rappers alone would not be commercial enough. In 2012, he added some vocalists to the mix. Enter Jeon Jungkook, Kim Taehyung (V) and Kim Seokjin (Jin). The final piece fell into place when talented modern dancer Park Jimin joined the team in summer 2012, just months before the final line-up for Bangtan Sonyeondan, meaning 'Bulletproof Boy Scouts', was confirmed. Jimin must have really impressed Hitman Bang in those auditions!

DEBUT TIME

Preparing to debut, as releasing your first song is known in the K-pop world, was not easy. Seven boys of different ages and from different backgrounds were thrown together in one dormitory, attending school during the day and practising hard in the evenings and often through the night. Tensions ran high and there were sometimes arguments and fights. But looking back, this difficult time forged a bond between those seven boys that now seems unbreakable – they are each other's closest friends and biggest supporters.

Finally, in the summer of 2013, it was time to debut: the album was recorded, the music video shot, the stage choreography perfected. On 12 June 2013, the boys made their debut on stage at a showcase in Seoul – but the next day was the one that really counted: they appeared live on television on two South Korean music shows, *M Countdown* and *Music Bank*, performing 'No More Dream' and 'We Are Bulletproof Pt. 2'.

STARS ON THE RISE

BTS weren't an overnight success story. The next few years were a lot of hard work, making albums and going on tour to meet their fans. Their first concert tour, 'The Red Bullet', began in Korea in October 2014. They performed for 5,000 devoted fans across three nights at a small concert hall in Seoul. Just over a year later, in

December 2015, they hit another huge milestone: entering the US Billboard 200 album chart with *The Most Beautiful Moment in Life Pt. 2*. This was a sign that their popularity outside Asia was on the rise, and that their new musical 'era' (a series of stylistically similar albums and singles) was resonating with fans.

Earlier that year they had achieved a different kind of victory: moving out of the cramped dorms where the seven of them shared one bedroom, and into more spacious accommodation where they had a whole *three* bedrooms between them. The oldest members, Jin and Suga, bunked up together, RM and Jungkook took another room, and J-Hope, Jimin and V shared the third.

2016 saw BTS building on their popularity at home and abroad, performing at KCON in the USA and taking a trip to Scandinavia for the first season of their reality TV series, *Bon Voyage*. At long last, they also won their first coveted *daesang* (grand prize) at the Melon Music Awards (MMAs) for 'Album of the Year' with *The Most Beautiful Moment in Life: Young Forever*, and a second *daesang* shortly after, at the Mnet Asian Music Awards (MAMAs) for 'Artist of the Year'.

The following year, BTS released 'Spring Day', a song that is still one of their most popular ever – it's barely left the charts in South Korea since it was released. Shortly afterwards, the boys went on tour again, visiting the USA, South America, Australia and East and Southeast Asia. In May 2017, while they were on tour, BTS made history once again by winning 'Top Social Artist' at the Billboard Music Awards (BBMAs), which is based on online social engagement (in other words, who's got the most dedicated fans). Canadian singer Justin Bieber had won every year since 2011, so BTS winning proved the dedication of their growing fanbase.

A NEW ERA

Life in BTS is pretty non-stop. As soon as the boys had finished their world tour, they were back in the studio preparing for another era. The release of *Love Yourself: Her* came with an unexpected surprise: an offer to perform at the American Music Awards (AMAs) in November 2017. When BTS brought the house down with an electric performance of 'DNA', they became the first Korean artists to ever grace the stage at the AMAs. They didn't know it then, but things were about to get even crazier – this was just the beginning.

RM

NAME:
KIM NAMJOON

AKA:
RM, RAP MONSTER, NAMU

D.O.B.:
12 SEPTEMBER 1994

BIRTHPLACE:
SEOUL, SOUTH KOREA

STAR SIGN:
VIRGO

CHINESE ZODIAC:
DOG

HEIGHT:
1.81 M (5 FT 11 IN)

As the leader of BTS, RM has a lot of responsibility on his shoulders. Recruited because of his talent as a rapper on the underground music scene in Korea, where he was part of a hip-hop crew called DNH (or DaeNamHyup), he is involved in the writing of almost every single BTS song, as well as doing a lot of production work.

BRIGHT BEGINNINGS

Born in Seoul, RM grew up in Ilsan, not far from the capital, with his parents and younger sister. His parents saw how bright he was at school, and wanted him to be a successful businessman – but the young Namjoon had other ideas. With a passion for hip-hop and rap, he would write lyrics and hide them among his schoolwork. His parents didn't approve, but he argued that even though he was smart – his grades put him at around 5000th (close to the top 1%) in the country – he was convinced he could be the #1 rapper in the country. Wouldn't they prefer to have a son who was #1 instead of #5000? The argument seems to have worked. Now, he's not only one of the best rappers in South Korea, but one of the best in the world!

RM is the most fluent English-speaker of the group, and he is often teased by his bandmates when he tells the story of how he learnt the language: by watching a boxset of *Friends* DVDs. He tends to take the lead in interviews outside Korea, and translates questions for the other boys. RM usually speaks English with an American accent, but when in the UK he sometimes puts on an adorable British accent instead.

RAP MONSTER

Passing his Big Hit Entertainment audition in 2010, Namjoon was the first member of the group that would become BTS. He chose the stage name Rap Monster, which was later shortened to RM. Suga soon joined him in the Big Hit dorms, and that's when the BTS magic really started.

LEADING THE GROUP

Despite what his early choice of stage name might indicate, RM is no monster. He's an intelligent, articulate man who loves wandering around art galleries, reading books, riding his bicycle along the Han River and tending to his bonsai trees – when he's not working hard writing lyrics, or even harder learning choreography. RM takes great care of the other members of BTS, as he takes his role as leader very seriously. He's always there for others to lean on or look to for support. He's also known for being one of the clumsiest members of the group, prone to breaking all sorts of things, and losing everything from his passport (when abroad on the first season of *Bon Voyage*) to his AirPods (33 pairs lost so far).

GOING SOLO

As well as all his work for BTS, RM is also a prolific solo artist, with two mixtapes and a whole string of collaborations to his name. His first mixtape, the hard-hitting *RM*, was released in 2015, and is about his insecurities as well as a response to people who criticized him. The second mixtape, *mono.*, is a much more mellow affair, full of introspective songs about loneliness. Aside from his mixtapes, RM's collaborated with everyone, from Lil Nas X (on 'Seoul Town Road', an 'Old Town Road' remix) and Fall Out Boy (on 'Champion') to Korean hip-hop legend Tiger JK (on 'Timeless') and singer-songwriter Younha (on 'Winter Flower'). And of course, he couldn't refuse a collaboration with his bandmate Suga's alter-ego Agust D, on 'Strange'. In 2021, RM released 'Bicycle' on SoundCloud – a soothing track about riding his bicycle to cheer himself up if he feels sad. It had to be 'Bicycle' and not 'Car', because RM still doesn't have his driving licence!

"Happiness is not something that you have to achieve. You can still feel happy during the process of achieving something."

"The labels of what being masculine is, is an outdated concept. It is not our intention to break it down. But if we are making a positive impact, we are very thankful. We live in an age where we shouldn't have those labels or have those restrictions."

"I think the biggest love is the love for oneself, so if you want to love others, you should love yourself first."

RM'S STYLE

RM's fashion has evolved a lot over the years, but he's always been stylish. A big fan of earthy, neutral colours and baggy fits, he's also been known to wear skirts without a second thought, and loves a colour co-ordinated sportswear look. He has said that style is all about attitude – it's not what you wear, it's how you wear it.

The most important thing is to just try things out and see what you like. He's tried many hairstyles and colours over the years, too, from bowl cuts to mullets and from highlighter yellow to cool silver, grape purple to bright ocean blue. He thinks silver suits him best, though.

ARMY

What's the secret to BTS's huge global success? Hard work, talent, brilliant music, great style ... All of these are important, but don't forget the not-so-secret ingredient: ARMY.

A GLOBAL FANBASE

Standing for 'Adorable Representative M.C. for Youth', ARMY is the name given to BTS's passionate, fiercely loyal fanbase. ARMY is an incredibly diverse fandom, representing all ages, genders and ethnicities around the world.

As much as ARMY love BTS, BTS love ARMY even more. Every time they win an award or get a song to #1 in the charts, BTS thank their fans. They know that it's only with ARMY's support that they've got to where they are today. In Los Angeles in November 2021, the band held their first concerts in front of an in-person audience since the outbreak of the Covid-19 pandemic in 2020. As they took to the stage, the boys talked about their fear that their fans would have got bored and moved on after nearly two years of being away. The deafening screams that echoed around the stadium proved just how unfounded that fear was.

BTS communicate with ARMY a lot on social media. They can be found posting photos on Twitter, answering questions and chatting about their days on V Live (a live video streaming app). They also leave messages on Weverse – a social networking app where BTS members post random thoughts or share exciting news. Any tweet posted from the @BTS_twt account racks up millions of likes within hours because ARMY are always enthusiastic to see everything BTS have to share.

GIVING BACK

The boys are a kind-hearted bunch who try to give back to the world. They regularly make charitable donations, usually without announcing it, but word often gets out. ARMY in turn make a lot of effort to match BTS's generosity. When BTS donated $1,000,000 to the Black Lives Matter movement, ARMY matched it with $1,000,000 of their own in under 24 hours – an incredible achievement.

On a smaller scale, ARMY often use the boys' birthdays as opportunities to fundraise and have together donated huge sums to good causes. It's clear that ARMY are a very generous collective.

SONGS FOR ARMY

It's not just in acceptance speeches that BTS express their love for ARMY – they write songs for their fans, too. Here are a few tracks which were inspired by the most devoted fanbase on the planet:

'2! 3!'
FROM *WINGS*

'PIED PIPER'
FROM *LOVE YOURSELF: HER*

'MAGIC SHOP'
FROM *LOVE YOURSELF: TEAR*

'MIKROKOSMOS'
FROM *MAP OF THE SOUL: PERSONA*

'MOON'
FROM *MAP OF THE SOUL: 7*

'WE ARE BULLETPROOF: THE ETERNAL'
FROM *MAP OF THE SOUL: 7*

SOCIAL ANIMALS

From the very beginning, BTS have valued being able to communicate with their fans directly. Here's how to connect with the boys online ...

TWITTER

@BTS_twt is the boys' personal, shared account where they post themselves.

@bts_bighit is the official company account for announcements and news.

● ● ● ● ● ● ● ●

YOUTUBE

Subscribe to the **BANGTANTV** channel to make sure you never miss a new music video or Bangtan Bomb.

● ● ● ● ● ● ● ●

TIKTOK

When BTS joined TikTok they almost broke the internet. Follow them **@bts_official_bighit** for fun and silly short videos.

● ● ● ● ● ● ● ●

V LIVE

Search for 'BTS' on V Live and enjoy hours of vlogs and other fun content, such as old episodes of *Run BTS* and *BTS Gayo*.

WEVERSE

Check BTS's Weverse feed for late-night ramblings and the boys teasing each other on their own posts. This is also where you will find episodes of *Run BTS*, *Bon Voyage*, *In the Soop* and *Learn Korean with BTS*.

● ● ● ● ● ● ● ●

INSTAGRAM

On Instagram, unlike Twitter, each of the boys has their own personal account. This is where their individual personalities really shine through.

RM is **@rkive**

Jin is **@jin**

Suga is **@agustd**

J-Hope is **@uarmyhope**

Jimin is **@j.m**

V is **@thv**

Jungkook is **@jungkook.97**

JIN

The oldest member of BTS, Jin originally wanted to be an actor – in fact, he was studying acting at university when he was spotted by a Big Hit scout.

CLOSE FAMILY

He grew up in a tight-knit family, with his parents and older brother, who he got on well with. Jin's easy-going nature endear him to both BTS and ARMY; he's always cracking jokes and making sure everyone is having a good time. He's supportive behind the scenes, too – RM has spoken about how, especially in the early days, he relied on Jin.

When he started out as a trainee, Jin was the only member who had no previous singing or dancing experience. He worked extra hard to keep up and his efforts paid off. Jin's vocals are often praised for their beautiful clarity, steadiness and strength of emotion – and how about those high notes?

When he's not working hard, Jin loves nothing more than vegging out at home and playing video games. It's definitely well-deserved!

SHY GUY

Jin's also known as 'Worldwide Handsome', a reference to his good looks. This is actually a nickname that he gave himself! This might seem big-headed, until you notice how red his ears go when he's getting too much attention. At heart, Jin's a shy guy who likes to exaggerate for comic effect ... although he really is very handsome.

NAME:
KIM SEOKJIN

AKA:
JIN, SEOKJINNIE,
WORLDWIDE HANDSOME

D.O.B.:
4 DECEMBER 1992

BIRTHPLACE:
ANYANG, SOUTH KOREA

STAR SIGN:
SAGITTARIUS

CHINESE ZODIAC:
MONKEY

HEIGHT:
1.79 M (5 FT 10 IN)

CHEF JIN

Jin loves to cook. He and Suga are the most competent in the kitchen, and you can see them take the reins in *Run BTS* cooking challenges, or when they're left to their own devices in the reality shows *In the Soop* or *Bon Voyage*. Jin also has a series of online videos known as 'Eat Jin', where he sits and eats while chatting with ARMY live on camera. For someone who loves good food, it must have been devastating for Jin to find out that he's allergic to both potatoes and garlic!

FREE TIME

Cooking isn't the only hobby that Jin and Suga share – they also go fishing together (or, as Suga revealed, he loves to go fishing with Jin because it makes Jin happy). But put Jin together with youngest member Jungkook and the more mature hobbies go out the window. Instead, you know chaos is on its way – like when Jungkook emptied an entire bottle of water over Jin in the middle of a concert!

SOLO TRACKS

While Jin doesn't produce as much solo music as some of the other members, the tracks that he shares on SoundCloud are adored by ARMY. These songs show Jin's more introspective side. 'Abyss', released during the Covid-19 pandemic, is a song about feeling alone, burned out and unworthy of praise. 'Tonight', a song about the fear of losing those you love, was inspired by the deaths of Jin's pet sugar gliders. 'Yours' was recorded for the soundtrack of the K-drama *Jirisan*. This similarly mournful tune showcases his beautiful voice superbly.

CHEERY TUNES

Jin's solo tracks on BTS albums tend to be more upbeat. 'Epiphany' has an uplifting message of self-love, while 'Moon' is a peppy, up-tempo track about how much Jin loves and admires ARMY. And then, of course, there's 'Super Tuna', released as a surprise on Jin's birthday in 2021. The song is about his love of fishing and is accompanied by a hilarious music video.

"If you receive, you have to give, that's the rule of life."

"Your presence can give happiness. I hope you remember that."

"My good luck charm is my face."

JIN'S STYLE

Known for his love of comfy co-ords, Jin looks just as good dressed down as up. With his model-like looks, he pulls off sleek designer suits with ease, but in his downtime, he likes to wear tracksuit bottoms and hoodies. He's also been known to dress a little, well, ridiculously – in order to entertain, of course. Who could forget his pink-and-white checked shirt, red tie, denim shorts and straw cowboy hat combo, worn while sightseeing in Malta during *Bon Voyage*? It was so attention-grabbing it prompted him to ask J-Hope, "Are you ashamed of me?" Ever honest, J-Hope replied, "A little, yes".

RECORDS & AWARDS

BTS just can't seem to stop breaking records (often their own!) and winning awards. They already have over 20 official Guinness World Records – enough to get them into the Guinness World Records Hall of Fame – and a whole host of other trophies besides. Here are just a few.

'DYNAMITE' BROKE THE RECORD FOR THE MOST WEEKS AT #1 ON THE BILLBOARD DIGITAL SONG SALES CHART — THE SMASH-HIT SONG RULED THE CHARTS FOR 18 WEEKS.

'BUTTER' PREMIERED ON YOUTUBE IN MAY 2021 TO AN AUDIENCE OF 3,900,000 VIEWERS — BREAKING THE WORLD RECORD FOR THE MOST VIEWERS FOR A YOUTUBE PREMIERE.

BTS HOLD THE RECORD FOR THE FASTEST ACCOUNT TO REACH 1,000,000 FOLLOWERS ON TIKTOK.

BTS ARE THE MOST STREAMED GROUP ON SPOTIFY, WITH TENS OF BILLIONS OF STREAMS — EVEN MORE IMPRESSIVE WHEN YOU REMEMBER THAT SPOTIFY ONLY LAUNCHED IN SOUTH KOREA IN 2021.

IN 2020, THE BOYS SWEPT THE BOARD AT THE MNET ASIAN MUSIC AWARDS (AKA THE MAMAS), BAGGING 'ARTIST OF THE YEAR', 'WORLDWIDE ICON OF THE YEAR', 'BEST MALE GROUP', 'SONG OF THE YEAR' AND 'ALBUM OF THE YEAR', TO NAME A FEW.

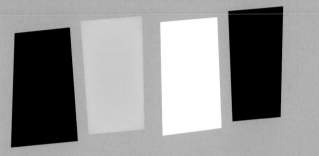

SOME OF THE AMAZING ARTISTS WHO HAVE BEEN LUCKY ENOUGH TO COLLABORATE WITH BTS INCLUDE MEGAN THEE STALLION, COLDPLAY, NICKI MINAJ, TROYE SIVAN, HALSEY, ED SHEERAN AND STEVE AOKI.

THE BEST-SELLING ALBUM EVER IN SOUTH KOREA IS BTS'S *MAP OF THE SOUL: 7*, WHICH HAS SOLD OVER 4.5 MILLION COPIES.

THE BANGTAN BOYS ALSO HOLD THE RECORD FOR MOST VIEWED YOUTUBE VIDEO IN THE FIRST 24 HOURS — A RECORD THAT THEY KEEP SETTING AND BREAKING WITH EACH NEW MUSIC VIDEO THEY RELEASE.

AT THE AMERICAN MUSIC AWARDS (AMAS), BTS WON 'FAVOURITE DUO OR GROUP POP/ROCK' IN 2019 AND 2020, AND 'TOUR OF THE YEAR' IN 2019 AS WELL. THEY'VE ALSO BEEN NOMINATED FOR TWO GRAMMYS!

SUGA

NAME:
MIN YOONGI

AKA:
SUGA, AGUST D, GLOSS

D.O.B.:
9 MARCH 1993

BIRTHPLACE:
DAEGU, SOUTH KOREA

STAR SIGN:
PISCES

CHINESE ZODIAC:
ROOSTER

HEIGHT:
1.74 M (5 FT 9 IN)

BTS's formidable rapper, genius producer and lyrical wizard Suga grew up in Daegu, South Korea, with his parents and older brother. His family didn't have much money when he was young, and they didn't think pursuing music was a sensible choice. But the young Min Yoongi was set on following his dreams, and worked hard producing beats and writing lyrics alongside his schoolwork and part-time jobs.

BIG BREAK

Suga's break came when, aged 18, he attended an audition for a new hip-hop group that Bang Si-hyuk was putting together. Although Suga came second in the audition, Hitman Bang was impressed enough to take a chance on the budding rapper, and invited him to join Big Hit as a trainee. Suga hasn't forgotten the promise he was made back then – that he wouldn't have to dance!

From the earliest days of BTS, Suga has been one of the driving forces behind their musical style, not only writing lyrics but creating beats and producing songs, too. He learned to play piano when he was a kid – that's what his solo track 'First Love' from the album *Wings* is about – but since then, he's also taught himself to play guitar and drums. Making music is his passion – as well as his work with BTS, Suga is prolific as a solo artist, under the name Agust D. His first mixtape, *Agust D*, was released in 2016, and his second, *D-2*, was released in 2020.

SING MORE

The rapper has even started occasionally singing. When Suga asked mentors for tips on how to improve his singing, he was told not to try to sing *better* – just to sing *more*. He's in demand as a writer and producer for other artists, too, having worked with Halsey, MAX, IU, Suran, Epik High, Lee So-ra and Heize.

COOL HEAD

Aside from his musical contributions to the group, Suga is loved by the other members for his unflappable attitude and caring ways. Behind his occasionally grumpy façade, he's a big softie who loves nothing more than cooking a nourishing meal for the members, or fixing whatever RM has just broken. He's also got a wicked sense of humour, and you can often see the others cracking up at his deadpan delivery in episodes of *Run BTS* or in 'Bangtan Bombs' on YouTube. And although Suga can appear a little reserved behind the scenes – he is often spotted napping – see him on stage and you'll understand how he got his fierce reputation.

SPEAKING UP

In interviews and in the lyrics he writes, Suga has always been open about the struggles he has faced with his mental health and how he wants to help others who are going through a tough time – he's even talked about studying to become a therapist. He always says he hopes that his music can be a comfort to people, and he encourages anyone who is struggling to talk about their problems.

TRIVIA MASTER

Suga is also a never-ending source of interesting facts and trivia, and is the one the other boys turn to when they need to know something a bit obscure. While RM might be the one who does the majority of the speaking in English-language interviews, fans are pretty convinced that Suga is a lot more fluent in English than he lets on. Smart, compassionate and talented – that's Min Yoongi!

"I want my music to become that light for those in the dark. I want them to heal from it and find the courage to step forward again."

"Age and gender, nationality and religion, what language you use – all of that isn't important to me."

"I want people to get positive energy from our music."

SUGA'S STYLE

Suga's main priority when it comes to clothes is comfort. He likes relaxed, loose-fitting T-shirts, fuzzy jumpers, comfy tracksuit bottoms and trainers or chunky sandals – usually in black. He also loves a hat and is often seen in beanies, bucket hats and baseball caps. And he's keen on accessories, too, with a large collection of rings, bracelets and necklaces to add a bit of bling to his low-key outfits, as well as headbands galore and a whole array of statement sunglasses. He's had a whole rainbow of hair colours, from mint green to blushing pink, silver grey to deep rich red, icy blond to jet black and everything in between – and of course, he suits every single one.

J-HOPE

NAME:
JUNG HOSEOK

AKA:
J-HOPE, HOBI, HOB-AH

D.O.B.:
18 FEBRUARY 1994

BIRTHPLACE:
GWANGJU, SOUTH KOREA

STAR SIGN:
AQUARIUS

CHINESE ZODIAC:
DOG

HEIGHT:
1.77 M (5 FT 10 IN)

You're his hope, he's your hope, he's J-Hope! J-Hope, real name Jung Hoseok, is the self-appointed sunshine of BTS. Affectionately referred to as Hobi by his fellow members and fans alike, this talented rapper and incredibly talented dancer is vital to the makeup of the group.

DANCE CAPTAIN

Growing up in Gwangju, in the southwest of South Korea, the young Hoseok had a passion for street dance. He took dance classes at Gwangju Music Academy and performed as part of the under-ground dance team Neuron, winning prizes and acclaim, including first place in a national dance competition when he was 14.

His amazing dance skills won him a place in BTS, where he took up the mantle of 'dance captain'. J-Hope is the one the others look to if they're struggling to learn a tricky bit of choreography, and he's always happy to help. When J-Hope joined Big Hit, he didn't have any singing or rapping experience. Luckily, bandmate Suga took him under his wing and helped J-Hope learn how to rap. Listening to his smooth, effortless flow now, you'd never know he was a rookie when he joined!

RAY OF HOPE

J-Hope didn't find the trainee years easy – in fact, he nearly quit before BTS's debut. RM convinced him to stay, and thank goodness he did. BTS wouldn't be the same without their resident sunshine. Suga sometimes refers to J-Hope as his personal battery, saying he needs to be recharged by his cheerful presence. J-Hope cares about making sure all of the members are happy, and that ARMY are happy, too.

MULTI-TALENTED

J-Hope loves to show off his dance skills on stage and off, sometimes recording special 'Hope on the Street' videos where he pulls off some jaw-dropping moves. But it's not just dancing he's known for; he's a prolific songwriter, having a hand in much of BTS's discography, and working on his own solo music, too. His 2018 mixtape, *Hope World*, is as bright and bubbly as he is, with upbeat but laid-back tracks such as 'Daydream' and 'Airplane', as well as the moodier 'Blueside' showing that even the sunshine can have blue days. J-Hope's 2019 collaboration with Mexican-American artist Becky G, 'Chicken Noodle Soup', sampled the 2006 song of the same name that both J-Hope and Becky G grew up listening and learning to dance to. A super-fun track sung in Korean, Spanish and English, the accompanying dance was infectious. Funky chicken, anyone?

LOVE TO SHARE

J-Hope is generally a private person, but he reveals his hopes, fears and the things he loves through his music. His *Wings* solo track, 'Mama', is about how much he loves his mum and appreciates the sacrifices she made for him while he was growing up. And his solo on *LY: Answer*, 'Trivia: Just Dance', is about – that's right – his love of dancing.

"You are the leader of your own life."

"The next attempt may not be perfect, but the second is better than the first, and the third is even better than the second."

"When things get tough, look at the people who love you! You will get energy from them."

J-HOPE'S STYLE

J-Hope clearly has fun with fashion – the brighter or more ridiculous (to some) the item of clothing, the more likely it is you'll see him sporting it. He loves bright, fun streetwear, and he definitely doesn't want to blend into the crowd. Generally, he's a fan of big, oversize pieces in bold colours and patterns, and loves to accessorize. He's often seen out and about with a little pouch or small bag of some kind, as well as plenty of jewellery. His earrings are all clip-on, though, as he doesn't have his ears pierced. While he's adventurous with his clothes, J-Hope's more conservative with his hair, tending to stick to shades of black, brown and auburn, not far from his natural colour. Though he does occasionally stray to a cherry red or an icy white blond, with breathtaking results.

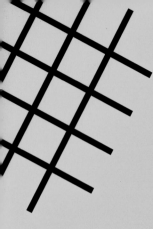

GOOD DEEDS

Since their debut days, BTS have always tried to help those in need. Here are just some of the ways the boys have given back to the world.

IN 2015, BACK WHEN BTS WERE STILL A RELATIVELY NEW GROUP, THEY DONATED SEVEN TONS OF RICE TO CHARITY TO HELP FEED THE HUNGRY.

IN 2020, THEY DONATED $1,000,000 TO THE BLACK LIVES MATTER MOVEMENT, WHICH STANDS AGAINST RACIST VIOLENCE.

THEY FUNDED 'CONNECT, BTS', A SERIES OF MAJOR PUBLIC ART INSTALLATIONS BY INDEPENDENT ARTISTS ALL OVER THE WORLD. BTS ARE PASSIONATE ABOUT ACCESS TO ART AND SUPPORTING ARTISTS.

THE 'LOVE MYSELF' CAMPAIGN, FOR WHICH BTS PARTNERED WITH UNICEF, HAS RAISED MILLIONS OF DOLLARS TO HELP END VIOLENCE AGAINST CHILDREN. IT AIMS TO IMPROVE THE SELF-ESTEEM AND WELLBEING OF YOUNG PEOPLE AROUND THE WORLD.

BTS HAVE BEEN INVITED TO SPEAK AT THE UN NOT ONCE, NOT TWICE, BUT THREE TIMES. THEY HAVE USED THEIR PLATFORM TO SPREAD A MESSAGE OF SELF-ACCEPTANCE AND STANDING AGAINST PREJUDICE.

BTS DONATED $1,000,000 TO LIVE NATION'S 'CREW NATION' CAMPAIGN TO SUPPORT PEOPLE WHO WORK IN THE LIVE MUSIC INDUSTRY DURING THE COVID-19 PANDEMIC, WHEN ALL LIVE MUSIC EVENTS WERE CANCELLED.

INSPIRED BY BTS' GENEROSITY, ARMY OFTEN USE THE BOYS' BIRTHDAYS AS OPPORTUNITIES TO FUNDRAISE. AS A COLLECTIVE, THEY DONATED RICE TO HUNGRY FAMILIES IN J-HOPE'S HOME-TOWN AND RAISED OVER $54,000 TO PROVIDE PROSTHETIC HANDS FOR THOSE IN NEED IN HONOUR OF V'S BIRTHDAY.

BIRTHDAY DONATIONS

As well as all their collective donations and advocacy work, BTS have a habit of individually donating to good causes on their birthdays. Here are just a few of their birthday donations:

RM donated 100,000,000 KRW (approximately $85,000) to a centre for hearing-impaired children to help with their musical education.

•

JIN has donated at least 100,000,000 KRW to UNICEF, becoming part of their Honors Club in 2019.

•

SUGA donated 100,000,000 KRW to a medical centre in his hometown of Daegu to support children with cancer.

•

J-HOPE donated 150,000,000 KRW (approximately $125,000) to ChildFund Korea to help children with vision and hearing impairments.

•

JIMIN donated 100,000,000 KRW to the Green Umbrella Child Foundation, a Korean charity that helps underprivileged children.

•

Fans are certain that **V** and **JUNGKOOK** have been similarly generous, but are just better at keeping their donations quiet – kind *and* humble!

RUN BTS

It's no secret that BTS are loved for their personalities as well as their music, and where better to see them shine than in their very own variety series, *Run BTS*?

Run BTS aired its first episode in 2015 and has been a firm fan favourite ever since. In over 150 episodes, fans can watch the boys doing everything from bungee jumping to dog training, kimchi-making to karaoke and interior design to table tennis. Episodes can be watched on V Live and Weverse. Here are some of the highlights.

EPISODE 23: 'PET FRIENDS'

This episode sees the boys paired up with a variety of adorable dogs, who they have to compete with in an agility course. If you love dogs, this is one to watch – V and his corgi, Chopa, are sooo cute!

EPISODE 24: 'BTS VS. ZOMBIES'

Not for the easily spooked, this episode pits the boys against some scary zombies while they try to make it through an obstacle course and solve puzzles – not easy when there are monsters all around you. Would you try to fight the zombies, like Suga, or run away screaming, like J-Hope?

EPISODES 83–85: 'SUMMER OUTING'

What happens when you put BTS on a huge inflatable obstacle course on a lake? Chaos, of course. Slipping and sliding, falling into the lake, all the boys teaming up against Jungkook, and Jungkook still winning ... these episodes have it all.

EPISODES 102–103: 'KING OF AVATAR COOK'

We all know that Suga and Jin are pretty handy in the kitchen, but the other members are a bit of a disaster in this area – so what could be more amusing than watching an increasingly frustrated Suga and Jin try to instruct their teams to cook simple dishes via walkie-talkie from the control room? It's unfortunate that sugar and salt look so similar ...

EPISODES 104–105: 'PHOTO EXHIBITION'

From a random assortment of clothes and accessories, BTS must create brand-new outfits, and draw lots to see who has to wear what. Jungkook's eventual outfit is truly not to be missed – there aren't many people who could pull that off!

... AND BEYOND

As well as *Run BTS* and *In the Soop* (see page 56), there are loads of other brilliant bits of on-screen BTS content – here are some ones to watch.

V LIVE

BTS love to share their thoughts and feelings directly with their fans, and often 'go live' on vlive.tv. Alone or as a group, the boys chat about their day, celebrate birthdays, do random activities (J-Hope making friendship bracelets for the other members was so cute!) or talk about new music.

BTS GAYO

This variety show was short but sweet at just 21 episodes split across two seasons in 2015 and 2017, with the boys competing against each other in various Korean-pop-culture-related activities. If you've ever wanted to watch BTS attempt girl-group dances or re-enact famous scenes from K-dramas, this is the show for you.

BON VOYAGE

Scandinavia, Hawaii, Malta, New Zealand ... these far-flung destinations are the setting for all sorts of unsupervised chaos as BTS travel the world and look after themselves. Who could forget RM losing his passport and having to leave early in season 1, or seeing Jin's, er, unique sense of fashion embarrass J-Hope in season 3?

BANGTAN BOMBS

Posted frequently on BTS's YouTube channel, these videos are a great behind-the-scenes look at everything BTS get up to – from messing around in dressing rooms to practising hard for new performances.

BURN THE STAGE / BRING THE SOUL / BREAK THE SILENCE

This trio of documentary films from 2018, 2019 and 2020 is a brilliant way to get to know the boys. Following them on three of their sell-out world tours, you can see all the ups and downs of superstardom, the offstage struggles and the onstage magic.

TALK SHOW APPEARANCES

Of course, as well as all their own content, BTS are often guests on well-known talk shows, hosted by Jimmy Fallon, James Corden and Graham Norton, to name just a few. You can always find the interviews, challenges and performances on YouTube.

JIMIN

NAME:
PARK JIMIN

AKA:
CHIM CHIM, BABY MOCHI,
MANGGAETTEOK

D.O.B.:
13 OCTOBER 1995

BIRTHPLACE:
BUSAN, SOUTH KOREA

STAR SIGN:
LIBRA

CHINESE ZODIAC:
PIG

HEIGHT:
1.74 M (5 FT 9 IN)

BTS without Jimin is unimaginable – but he was the last member to join as a trainee, just months before debut. His beautiful vocals and graceful dancing are a fundamental part of BTS's DNA, so it was lucky that his dance teacher convinced him to audition. He considered several stage names, including Baby J and Young Kid, but in the end he stuck with his own name, Jimin.

DREAMY DANCER

Jimin grew up in the port city of Busan with his parents and younger brother. He did well at school and discovered a passion for dancing at a young age. This led him to enrol at the Busan High School of Arts to major in modern dance. You can see the elegance he learnt there shine through in the street-style hip-hop choreography of early BTS. As the group evolved, Jimin got more opportunities to show off his dance skills. Watch the breathtaking 'Black Swan' performances to see his talent in action.

He might look like an angel, but Jimin is one of the most mischievous members of BTS. He loves to stir up trouble and play pranks on the other members, especially when they're playing games for *Run BTS*. That said, he's also the member that the others go to with their troubles, as he's always there to listen.

RECORD-BREAKING

Jimin is a perfectionist – it took him ages to release his first self-written solo song, 'Promise', as he wanted it to be just right. Originally a much darker song, it became a wholesome and uplifting track about overcoming life's obstacles. When it was finally released, the track broke SoundCloud's record for most streams in 24 hours. His other solo songs range from the dramatic 'Lie' to the bubbly 'Serendipity'. And, of course, there's his duet with V, 'Friends', which the two pals wrote together about their firm and occasionally rocky friendship. Their clash over dumplings, known as the 'dumpling incident', is even referenced in their song.

HIGH PRESSURE

Always aiming to be the best he can be means that Jimin sometimes puts too much pressure on himself. This was especially true of his time as a trainee, when he would often only get a few hours of sleep because he was practising into the night and attending school during the day. We're glad he's got a healthier work–life balance these days. Jimin loves nothing more than being reminded that he really is a brilliant performer who captivates the entire audience whenever he takes centre stage.

NOT SO SERIOUS

While his presence is often serious and focused, Jimin can be very funny when he lets go a little, especially on episodes of *Run BTS*. Who could forget the classic "carbonara! lachimolala?" lip-reading mix-up, when the boys were playing a whispering game? Or Jimin's cheeky expression in the hands-on-hips photo secretly taken by Jungkook during a DIY fashion photoshoot? Jimin can often be caught on camera bickering with Suga or winding RM up, because he knows ARMY love to see these silly moments and he's committed to giving the fans what they want.

"Genuine laughter is so much better than forcing a smile or frowning, so I hope the days with lots of genuine laughter come sooner."

"Remember there is a person here in Korea, in the city of Seoul, who understands you."

"Don't give up on yourself. Take care of yourself and take control of your life."

JIMIN'S STYLE

"Cutie, sexy, lovely" – Jimin's description of his own style is hard to argue with. One of the most elegantly dressed members, Jimin loves to look chic, often wearing a monochrome outfit with his signature black Chelsea boots and dangly silver earrings. But he's not afraid of dressing down, either, in skinny jeans and cozy hoodies.

He's tried all sorts of hair colours over the years, from bleach blond to candyfloss pink and tangerine orange to jet black. But one thing is a constant with Jimin's hair – his habit of running his hand through it and pushing his fringe back (which the others love to tease him for).

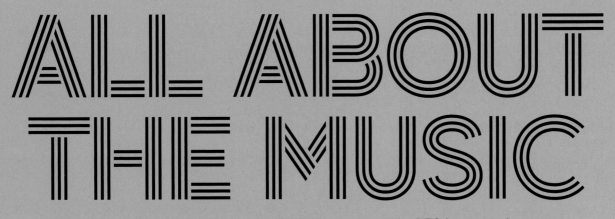

ALL ABOUT THE MUSIC

From hip-hop to power ballads and EDM to emo rock, BTS have tried pretty much every genre you can think of. With such a huge discography, it can be hard to know where to begin – so here's a run-down of all their music so far.

2 COOL 4 SKOOL – JUNE 2013

BTS's debut single album, *2 Cool 4 Skool* is a statement of intent. With nine tracks, including the singles 'No More Dream' and 'We Are Bulletproof Pt. 2', it's half an hour of energetic hip-hop dealing with themes of prejudice, societal pressure and anxiety about the future.

MV TO WATCH: 'No More Dream' has baby-faced Bangtan trying to look meaner than they are, crashing into the music industry on a big yellow school bus.

O!RUL8,2? – SEPTEMBER 2013

Continuing the 'School Trilogy', this EP features the singles 'N.O' and 'Attack on Bangtan'. Showcasing their musical versatility, there are hardcore hip-hop tracks such as 'Paldogangsan' and soft, sweet love songs like 'Coffee', as well as 'BTS Cypher Pt. 1', where the three rappers show off their skills.

MV TO WATCH: 'N.O' shows BTS rebelling against a controlling, dystopian school system – everybody say NO!

SKOOL LUV AFFAIR – FEBRUARY 2014

This album features the catchy 'Boy in Luv' and adorable 'Just One Day', as well as Suga-produced 'Tomorrow' and the next of the rap line's cyphers, 'BTS Cypher Pt. 2: Triptych'. The 'Special Addition' version also features 'Miss Right' and instrumental versions of some songs.

MV TO WATCH: Although 'Boy in Luv' is the lead single, watch 'Just One Day' if you want to see a softer side of the Bangtan boys.

DARK & WILD – AUGUST 2014

Their first full-length studio album, this brings BTS's earliest musical era to a close. Though the two singles, 'Danger' and 'War of Hormone', are dark and wild, BTS continue to show their softer side, with '24/7=Heaven' and 'Embarrassed'. With another fiery cypher, 'BTS Cypher Pt. 3: Killer', the funky 'Look Here' and moody 'Rain', there's something for all moods and tastes.

MV TO WATCH: 'Danger' is stylish and angsty, but 'War of Hormone' is where the real fun is – the video is full of silliness, and some seriously punky outfits.

THE MOST BEAUTIFUL MOMENT IN LIFE PT. 1 – APRIL 2015

This series of albums – often referred to as 'HYYH' after the Korean name, *Hwayangyeonhwa* (which roughly translates to 'the most beautiful moment in life') – marks a shift away from the group's debut hip-hop-heavy sound. Lead single 'I Need U' has the boys expressing their emotional vulnerability, while second single 'Dope' shows they haven't forgotten their musical roots.

MV TO WATCH: 'I Need U' is the first music video set in the 'BU', or Bangtan Universe. This high concept fictional timeline allows the group to explore often dark concepts and emotions, while being able to separate the members from the 'characters' they play.

THE MOST BEAUTIFUL MOMENT IN LIFE PT. 2 – NOVEMBER 2015

Continuing the HYYH era, the lead single 'Run' is a catchy song which encourages pushing on towards your goals, even if you get knocked down. BTS also go conceptual with 'Whalien 52', a song inspired by the real-life story of the 'world's loneliest whale', who sings at a frequency of 52hz – too high-pitched for it to communicate with other whales. Fan-favourite 'Baepsae', aka 'Silver Spoon', is a socially conscious song about the inequalities many in BTS's generation face.

MV TO WATCH: 'Run' continues the BU storyline, and shows the boys having fun at a house party before getting into trouble with the authorities.

THE MOST BEAUTIFUL MOMENT IN LIFE: YOUNG FOREVER – MAY 2016

BTS's first compilation album contains new singles, including the energetic 'Fire' and the tropical house EDM 'Save Me', as well as 'Epilogue: Young Forever'.

MV TO WATCH: Shot in one take, 'Save Me' shows the boys performing intense choreography on a rainy windswept beach. Behind-the-scenes footage shows just how freezing cold and wet they were after filming!

WINGS – OCTOBER 2016

Inspired by Hermann Hesse's novel *Demian*, this is BTS's first concept album, and also the first to feature solo tracks by each of the members. Lead single 'Blood Sweat & Tears' is about resisting temptation, whereas '21st Century Girl' and '2! 3!' bring some upbeat pop to the table.

MV TO WATCH: 'Blood Sweat & Tears' is a visual feast. The boys wear stunning outfits and dance in a deserted museum full of famous art.

YOU NEVER WALK ALONE – FEBRUARY 2017

This reissue album features all of the songs from *Wings*, plus new singles 'Spring Day' and 'Not Today', as well as 'A Supplementary Story: You Never Walk Alone'. 'Spring Day' is one of BTS's most popular songs ever – in some ways, it is their 'coming of age' song, revealing a new emotional and musical maturity.

MV TO WATCH: Inspired by both Bong Joon-ho's film *Snowpiercer* and Ursula K Le Guin's philosophical novella *The Ones Who Walk Away from Omelas*, 'Spring Day' is a beautiful music video, perfectly complementing the wistful mood of the song.

LOVE YOURSELF: HER
– SEPTEMBER 2017

The start of another new era, this EP shows a more pop-focused side to BTS. Upbeat EDM pop-led single 'DNA' is joined by the sweet and catchy 'Dimple', and the teasing 'Pied Piper'. It's not all cute, though – 'MIC Drop' features the heavy basslines and quickfire rapping that BTS are known and loved for.

MV TO WATCH: While the bubblegum-bright colours of 'DNA' are irresistible, the Steve Aoki remix of 'MIC Drop' came with a very stylish music video.

LOVE YOURSELF: TEAR
– MAY 2018

Continuing the 'Love Yourself' era but taking a much darker approach to it, lead single 'Fake Love' expresses the angst and heartbreak of a love story that isn't working out. But *Tear* isn't all gloom: 'Love Maze', 'Magic Shop' and 'Anpanman' provide some welcome brightness. The jazzy '134340' (named after Pluto's 'minor-planet designation number', of course) contrasts its upbeat sound with sad lyrics about the end of a relationship. RM raps about how his heart is 248 degrees below zero – the same temperature as it is on Pluto.

MV TO WATCH: While 'Fake Love' is a stunning, baroque music video, the video for the Japanese version of 'Airplane Pt. 2' (a sequel to 'Airplane' from J-Hope's solo mixtape) is a new style for BTS, with a Latin pop vibe.

LOVE YOURSELF: ANSWER
– AUGUST 2018

Bringing the 'Love Yourself' era to a close, this compilation album features songs from *LY: Her* and *LY: Tear*, as well as new solo tracks and a full-length version of Jungkook's 'Euphoria'. 'IDOL', the lead single, combines traditional Korean musical instruments, South African dance music and electronica with BTS's own distinctive flair.

MV TO WATCH: Matching the intensity of the song itself, the video for 'IDOL' is vivid. Featuring elements of *pansori* – traditional Korean musical storytelling – along with loud suits and wacky visual effects, this video makes a real impact.

MAP OF THE SOUL: PERSONA
– APRIL 2019

The dawn of yet another era, this EP is inspired by the theories of Swiss psychiatrist and psychoanalyst Carl Jung. The introspective but upbeat opening track, 'Intro: Persona', has RM wondering what his purpose in life is. This is followed by the bouncy lead single 'Boy with Luv', featuring Halsey. The poppy R&B track 'HOME' and closing rap-rock track 'Dionysus' reveal another new musical direction for BTS.

MV TO WATCH: 'Intro: Persona' introduces the 'persona', 'shadow' and 'ego' concepts from Jung's psychological theories.

MAP OF THE SOUL: 7
– FEBRUARY 2020

Featuring several songs from *MOTS: Persona*, this album also includes solo tracks by each member, as well as rap-line and vocal-line songs, 'UGH!' and '00:00 (Zero O'Clock)', and, for the first time, three subunit tracks – Jin, J-Hope and Jungkook teaming up for 'Jamais Vu', 'Friends' sung by Jimin and V, and 'Respect' by RM and Suga. And not forgetting lead single 'ON', a rousing anthem full of horns and drums.

MV TO WATCH: 'Black Swan' is a haunting song about the fear of losing your artistic passion, and its music video sees BTS performing ballet-inspired choreography. An alternative version of the music video features a Slovenian modern dance troupe performing to an orchestral remix of the track.

BE – NOVEMBER 2020

Written and released during the Covid-19 pandemic, *BE* is an introspective and often melancholy album, dealing with themes of isolation and loneliness, but also comfort and hope. Lead single 'Life Goes On' is a gentle track about persevering through hardships, while 'Blue & Grey' is an honest look at the feelings of loneliness the pandemic caused. The retro, funky 'Telepathy' is about BTS looking forward to a time when they can meet ARMY again, and the old-school hip-hop 'Dis-ease' is about feeling alienated. Also included is the English-language smash-hit 'Dynamite'.

MV TO WATCH: The soothing video for 'Life Goes On' was directed by none other than BTS's own Jungkook. Its relaxed, gentle mood fits the song perfectly.

BUTTER – JUNE 2021

The undisputed hit of summer 2021, BTS's second English-language single topped the charts for months on end. Released as a physical single album as well as a digital download, the physical version also included the Ed Sheeran-penned 'Permission to Dance' – an upbeat English song about dancing your troubles away. In August 2021, BTS released a remix of 'Butter' with American rapper Megan Thee Stallion.

MV TO WATCH: Breaking all the YouTube records that BTS themselves set, the music video for 'Butter' is an explosion of slick choreography and retro outfits perfectly complementing the smooth (like butter) beats.

JAPANESE RELEASES
AND ORIGINAL SOUNDTRACKS

• • • • • • • • • •

WAKE UP – DECEMBER 2014

Their first Japanese-language release, this album contains versions of 'No More Dream', 'Boy in Luv' and 'Danger', plus new just-for-Japan tracks 'The Stars' and 'Wake Up'.

YOUTH – SEPTEMBER 2016

With Japanese versions of 'Run', 'Fire', 'Dope', 'Save Me' and more, as well as the Japanese-only 'For You', 'Wishing on a Star' and 'Good Day', this album showed BTS's Japanese fans that they hadn't forgotten about them.

FACE YOURSELF – APRIL 2018

'Don't Leave Me', 'Let Go' and 'Crystal Snow' were the new Japanese songs on this album, alongside Japanese versions of 'Blood Sweat & Tears', 'DNA', 'MIC Drop' and 'Spring Day'.

BTS WORLD: ORIGINAL SOUNDTRACK – JUNE 2019

This album, an accompaniment to the mobile game 'BTS World', contains seven instrumental themes, one for each member, as well as collaborations with Charli XCX, Zara Larsson and Juice WRLD.

MAP OF THE SOUL: 7 – THE JOURNEY – JULY 2020

With bubbly lead single 'Lights', as well as 'Stay Gold' and 'Your Eyes Tell' making up the new Japanese-only songs, this album also contains Japanese versions of 'Boy With Luv', 'Dionysus', 'Fake Love' and 'Black Swan'.

BTS, THE BEST – JUNE 2021

This is a Japanese compilation album of BTS's biggest hits in Japanese, and includes the heartfelt ballad 'Film Out', written by Jungkook. At 23 tracks, this is a brilliant way to get to know BTS's Japanese discography.

V

NAME:
KIM TAEHYUNG

AKA:
V, TAE, TAETAE, VANTE

D.O.B.:
30 DECEMBER 1995

BIRTHPLACE:
DAEGU, SOUTH KOREA

STAR SIGN:
CAPRICORN

CHINESE ZODIAC:
PIG

HEIGHT:
1.79 M (5 FT 10 IN)

Kim Taehyung never meant to end up in BTS. He went along to a Big Hit audition to support a friend, but a member of staff spotted him and persuaded him to try out. Taehyung was then invited to join Big Hit as a trainee. He moved from Daegu to Seoul, entering the Big Hit dorms and enrolling in a new school – where he would later be joined by Park Jimin.

SURPRISE STAR

Choosing the stage name V (for victory), he was all set to debut. But unlike the other boys, who all posted pre-debut vlogs and photos on social media, V was kept a secret. When V was finally revealed as the secret seventh member of BTS, he instantly gained legions of admirers.

Singing and dancing aren't his only professional talents. V has also dabbled in acting, including in a K-drama called *Hwarang: The Poet Warrior Youth*, where he became firm friends with actors Park Seo-joon and Park Hyung-sik. Along with Choi Woo-shik, who starred in the Oscar-winning film *Parasite*, and the rapper Peakboy, the group make up the 'Wooga Squad' (the name they gave their friendship group).

CREATIVE PURSUITS

Known for his creative nature, V plays several instruments (saxophone, piano, violin and trumpet), loves painting and is a keen photographer. He enjoys visiting art galleries and he's also got a sharp eye for fashion, often pulling off striking outfits. As BTS are House Ambassadors for Louis Vuitton, V has walked the runway at Seoul Fashion Week as a model, too.

I PURPLE YOU

V is an affectionate guy, and when he's not making up terms of endearment for ARMY – 'I purple you' (borahae) was his invention – he's looking after his adorable Pomeranian, Yeontan. He often posts on Weverse when he has trouble sleeping and shares his favourite songs with fans. V's a big jazz and blues fan, so he encourages ARMY to listen to music they might never have heard before.

SOLO SONGS

His bewitching baritone voice is vital to BTS's sound, but as well as being part of the vocal line, V has released several solo songs. His self-written SoundCloud tracks, such as the wistful love song 'Scenery', show a romantic side to V. Charming Christmas song 'Snow Flower' was written with his friend Peakboy. English-language track 'Winter Bear' is accompanied by a music video containing footage he shot on his travels. V also duetted with Jin on 'It's Definitely You' for the Hwarang soundtrack, and released 'Sweet Night' (another English-language track) for the soundtrack of the K-drama Itaewon Class.

RAP SKILLS

V also loves showing off his impressive rap skills. From living his dream, performing the rap line's 'Cypher Pt. 3', to doing his best renditions of 'Ddaeng' and 'UGH!', he takes every opportunity to prove he could take his place among the rappers.

"Whenever things get hard, stop for a while and look back and see how far you've come."

"Do you know what purple means? Purple is the last colour of the rainbow, so it means I will trust and love you for a long time."

"Things may feel a little difficult right now, but somewhere out there, luck and opportunity is waiting for you."

V'S STYLE

One of the most stylish members of BTS, V could easily make it as a catwalk model. His stunning looks, plus his discerning and eclectic taste, are a killer combination. He's a big fan of Gucci, and loves patterned shirts, wide-legged trousers and unusual silhouettes. He's also not afraid of 'feminine' styling, such as lace, ruffles and ribbons, and he absolutely loves to accessorize with delicate pearl earrings and flashy gemstone rings.

BTS FLY
(2020)

2020 started well for BTS with the announcement of another new album, *Map of the Soul: 7*, an upcoming tour and the pre-album release of 'Black Swan'.

At the end of January, the band shared the stage with the American rapper Lil Nas X in a genre-mashing performance at the Grammys – a dream come true. They also launched 'Connect, BTS', a global project involving 22 independent artists, aiming to 'redefine the relationship between art and music'.

COVID-19

By March, with the spread of Covid-19, BTS made the decision to postpone their tour indefinitely and moved things online. The boys set up 'Bang Bang Con', which was streamed for free on YouTube and featured two days of archive concert footage, spanning 2014–2019. 'Bang Bang Con' had such a cheering effect on ARMY that BTS soon announced a follow-up concert: 'Bang Bang Con The Live'. With 756,000 paying viewers in over 100 countries, the online event connected BTS and ARMY worldwide.

DEAR CLASS OF 2020

In June 2020, BTS spoke alongside the likes of Lady Gaga and Michelle and Barack Obama during a virtual graduation ceremony held for students missing their own ceremonies due to Covid-19, which was streamed live for all on YouTube.

The pandemic showed no signs of stopping, so BTS decided to try something they'd never done before; they released a song with lyrics entirely in English. The upbeat, disco-influenced track 'Dynamite' finally got them their first Billboard Hot 100 #1 in the USA, and it topped charts all over the world. As hoped, 'Dynamite' connected with their global fanbase and uplifted audiences across the globe.

VIRTUAL TOUR

In October, the boys put on another virtual concert, 'Map of the Soul ON:E', which featured the setlist, stage sets and costumes that had been planned for their postponed world tour. It may not have been the tour they had in mind, but almost a million viewers paid to watch BTS perform online. Delighted fans were greeted by band members through the 'ARMY on Air' system, which displayed viewers' faces on screens in the venue as they watched the show.

GRAMMY GLORY

The boys ended the year on a high when their chart-topping global sensation 'Dynamite' was nominated for 'Best Pop Duo/Group Performance' – their first Grammy nomination for music. Finally!

After sweeping up a bunch of trophies during the Korean awards season, BTS were ready for the challenges of 2021. When the Grammys arrived in March 2021, they may not have taken home the coveted award, but their live performance, streamed from Seoul, was the most talked-about of the show.

2020 HAD BEGUN WITH A BANG AND THIS TREND WAS SET TO CONTINUE THROUGH 2021.

JUNGKOOK

NAME:
JEON JUNGKOOK

AKA:
JK, KOOKIE, GGUK,
GOLDEN MAKNAE

D.O.B.:
1 SEPTEMBER 1997

BIRTHPLACE:
BUSAN, SOUTH KOREA

STAR SIGN:
VIRGO

CHINESE ZODIAC:
OX

HEIGHT:
1.78 M (5 FT 10 IN)

Jeon Jungkook grew up in Busan with his parents and older brother. As Busan is on the coast, Jungkook nearly took the stage name 'Seagull', but decided to keep his own name instead. Jungkook was only 15 when BTS made their debut, so ARMY have watched him grow from a cute, undeniably talented, but rather shy teenage boy to a pierced, tattooed and confident young man.

GOLDEN GUY

Nicknamed 'golden *maknae*' (*maknae* means 'youngest' in Korean), Jungkook is a multi-talented guy. Not only is he BTS's main vocalist, with a versatile voice, he's also a powerful dancer, and could have easily taken his place on BTS's rap line. You can hear him rapping on some early songs and he relishes the opportunity to steal one of the rapper's verses during live performances. On top of his performance skills, he enjoys making art, editing footage for short movies, playing video games and writing lyrics. He is also an accomplished athlete and he has a black belt in taekwondo! Whew...

Jungkook is the baby of the group, and all the members have a soft spot for him. When he's not messing around with Jimin and V, he can often be found causing mayhem with Jin. And it's no secret that Jungkook really looks up to RM; despite having been scouted by several bigger agencies, the reason he auditioned for Big Hit was because he thought RM was *so* cool.

SHIFTING STYLES

Jungkook has probably gone through the most dramatic transformation since his debut days. Though he always looked like a bit of an emo kid with his multiple ear piercings and floppy fringe, he has now had his eyebrow and lip pierced, and covered his right arm and hand in tattoos. But he's still the same sweet boy inside – if you spot his knuckle tattoo, you'll see it spells out 'ARMY'.

FOR THE FANS

Jungkook's love for ARMY isn't just expressed in his tattoos. In 2020, he released 'Still With You' on SoundCloud as a gift for his fans. The slow, jazzy ballad was a new direction for Jungkook and left fans eager for his much-anticipated solo mixtape. He also helped to write the lyrics for BTS's 'Magic Shop', which he hoped would be a comforting song for ARMY. His solo songs on BTS albums tend to be quite energetic, from 'Begin', about the influence the other members have had on his growth as a person, to the twinkly pop perfection of 'Euphoria'. The up-tempo yet introspective 'My Time' is a song about how growing up in BTS has (while being an incredible experience) prevented him from doing 'normal' things other young people take for granted.

BIG HEART

Growing up in the spotlight is never easy and can sometimes lead to young stars going off the rails. However, Jungkook is surrounded by a great support system. He often expresses how grateful he is for the love he receives from his fellow band members and from ARMY, too. Jungkook likes to show his gratitude, whether that's by outdoing himself on stage or hosting two-hour-long karaoke sessions on V Live. Jungkook is a boy with a lot of talent and even more heart – golden in every way.

"You can do whatever you want with your life."

"Effort makes you. You'll regret someday if you don't try your best now."

"We should try to respect and understand each other. We need to be considerate of others."

JUNGKOOK'S STYLE

More rockstar than idol, Jungkook loves an edgy look. In his younger years, he liked to wear white T-shirts, blue jeans and Timberland boots. But nowadays, he is often spotted in a black leather jacket over a baggy T-shirt, tight black jeans and big black boots. To match his all-black outfits, Jungkook usually keeps his natural dark hair colour, though he has dabbled in other shades. Cherry red and bright blue looked striking on him, and who could forget the time he dyed one half of his bleached hair red by himself? Jungkook has a distinct sense of style but he's not afraid to take risks.

ALL THE MEMBERS HAVING FUN WITH JUNGKOOK'S DOG, BAM.

JIMIN, V AND JUNGKOOK PLAYING BASKETBALL IN THE POURING RAIN AND SETTING AMBITIOUS GOALS TO ACHIEVE BEFORE BEING ALLOWED INSIDE ... THEY GOT SOAKED!

AN EXASPERATED SUGA YELLING, "WOODCARVING *HAJIMA!*" ("DON'T DO WOODCARVING!") AT NOTORIOUSLY CLUMSY RM.

IN THE SOOP

JIN RELAXING ON THE INFLATABLE UNICORN IN THE POOL.

BTS's hit reality show, *In the Soop* (*soop* is the Korean word for 'forest'), gives fans the opportunity to watch the boys relax, cook, try new hobbies, go on group adventures and generally take a break from their busy lives. Originally shown on the television network JTBC and online platform Weverse, each episode follows the boys in a beautiful remote location in the stunning Korean countryside.

The first season, filmed during the Covid-19 pandemic and released in August 2020, offered an alternative to BTS's earlier globetrotting reality show *Bon Voyage*. Following the success of the first season of *In the Soop*, and due to ongoing Covid-19 travel restrictions, a second season was filmed and released in October 2021.

Here are just some of the most memorable moments from both trips to the forest.

J-HOPE INDULGING HIS INNER KID BY SPENDING HOURS CONSTRUCTING A TOY PLANE AND A BOTTLE ROCKET.

MIN PD, AKA SUGA, RECORDING THE *IN THE SOOP* JINGLE, WITH THE HELP OF JUNGKOOK'S HILARIOUS AD LIBS.

V, STANDING UP IN A CANOE ON THE LAKE, SERENADING A BAFFLED RM WHO WAS BUSY PAINTING.

ALL THE BOYS HAVING FUN WITH THE KARAOKE MACHINE AND BELTING OUT CLASSIC KOREAN SONGS.

RM GLEEFULLY PLAYING WITH A REMOTE-CONTROL BOAT ON THE LAKE – AND INEVITABLY GETTING IT STUCK IN THE REEDS.

JIMIN PRANKING SCAREDY-CAT J-HOPE WHEN THEY EXPLORE AN EMPTY 'HAUNTED' HOUSE.

SUGA RUSTLING UP EVERYTHING FROM SPICY CHICKEN *DAKGALBI* TO AN ELABORATE *HANWOO* BEEF FEAST FOR THE OTHER MEMBERS.

V PLAYING HIS TRUMPET WHILE J-HOPE DANCED BY THE POOL.

JIN STARTING EVERY MORNING BY GRABBING A ROLLED-UP YOGA MAT TO SMACK THE PUNCHING BAG WITH.

SUGA, THE BASKETBALL PRO, TEACHING JIMIN HOW TO SHOOT HOOPS.

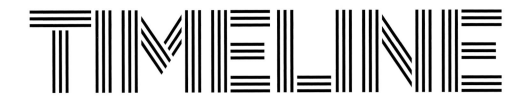

TIMELINE

2013

13 JUNE: the fresh-faced Bangtan boys debut with 'No More Dream' from *2 Cool 4 Skool*.

•

9 JULY: BTS's blossoming fanbase get their very own name, ARMY.

•

11 SEPTEMBER: *O!RUL8,2?* is released.

•

14 NOVEMBER: BTS win 'New Artist of the Year' at the MMAs.

2014

16 JANUARY: BTS win 'Rookie of the Year' at the GDAs.

•

12 FEBRUARY: *Skool Luv Affair* is released.

•

19 AUGUST: *Dark & Wild*, their first full-length album, is released.

•

17 OCTOBER: BTS play their first full-length solo concert at AX Hall in Seoul.

2015

29 APRIL: *The Most Beautiful Moment in Life Pt. 1* is released.

•

5 MAY: BTS get their first music-show win, *The Show Choice*, for 'I Need U'.

•

30 NOVEMBER: *The Most Beautiful Moment in Life Pt. 2* is released, and is their first entry on the Billboard 200 album chart.

2016

2 MAY: *The Most Beautiful Moment in Life: Young Forever* is released; lead single 'Fire' achieves their first 'all-kill', topping all 8 real-time Korean music charts.

•

10 OCTOBER: *WINGS* is released.

•

19 NOVEMBER: BTS finally win their first *daesang* (grand prize) with *The Most Beautiful Moment in Life: Young Forever*, taking the 'Album of the Year' trophy at the MMAs.

2017

13 FEBRUARY: *You Never Walk Alone* is released.

•

20 MAY: BTS win 'Top Social Artist' at the Billboard Music Awards.

•

3 SEPTEMBER: BTS join the fathers of K-pop, Seo Taiji and Boys, onstage for their 25th anniversary concert.

•

18 SEPTEMBER: *Love Yourself: Her* is released.

•

20 NOVEMBER: BTS become the first Korean group to perform at the American Music Awards.

2018

18 MAY: *Love Yourself: Tear* is released, debuting at #1 on the Billboard 200 album chart.

•

24 AUGUST: *Love Yourself: Answer* is released.

•

28 SEPTEMBER: BTS address the United Nations to speak about their 'Love Myself' UNICEF campaign.

•

24 OCTOBER: Each member of BTS is awarded an Order of Cultural Merit by the South Korean government – they are the youngest recipients ever.

2019

10 FEBRUARY: BTS attend their first Grammy Awards and present the 'Best R&B Album' award to H.E.R.

•

12 APRIL: *Map of the Soul: Persona* is released.

•

1 JUNE: BTS perform at London's iconic Wembley Stadium for two nights.

2020

26 JANUARY: BTS perform at the Grammys with Lil Nas X.

•

21 FEBRUARY: *Map of the Soul: 7* is released; 'ON' debuts at #4 on the Billboard Hot 100.

•

21 AUGUST: 'Dynamite' is released, becoming BTS's first Billboard Hot 100 #1.

•

23 SEPTEMBER: BTS return to speak at the UN.

•

23 NOVEMBER: 'Dynamite' is nominated for a Grammy.

2021

14 MARCH: BTS perform 'Dynamite' at the Grammys, streamed from Seoul.

•

21 MAY: 'Butter' is released and holds #1 spot on the Billboard Hot 100 for 10 weeks.

•

21 SEPTEMBER: BTS return to the UN for a third time; they give a speech and a performance.

•

24 OCTOBER: 'Permission to Dance On Stage' concert is live-streamed around the world.

•

23 NOVEMBER: BTS receive a second Grammy nomination for 'Butter'.

•

27 NOVEMBER: BTS play four sold-out nights in LA to their first live audience since the Covid-19 pandemic began.

2022

10 MARCH: BTS perform the first of three live performances at the Jamsil Olympic Stadium in Seoul – it was live-streamed across the world.

•

3 APRIL: BTS bring the house down with a heist-themed performance of 'Butter' at the Grammys in Las Vegas.

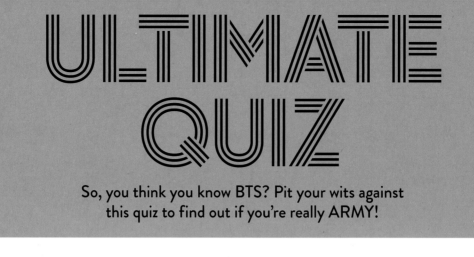

ULTIMATE QUIZ

So, you think you know BTS? Pit your wits against
this quiz to find out if you're really ARMY!

1. What does BTS stand for?

2. Which two members grew up in
the seaside city of Busan?

3. Which BTS album was the first to feature
individual members' solo tracks?

4. Which member has collaborated with Halsey,
MAX, Epik High, IU and Heize (and
many more) on their solo projects?

5. Which member plays the saxophone and
the trumpet, among other instruments?

6. Which BTS song was the first to chart on
the Billboard Hot 100 in America?

7. Which two members make up the '94 line'?

8. Which music video features a spoken word interlude,
quoting from the novel *Demian* by Herman Hesse?

9. Which member has kept sugar gliders as pets?

10. What does *borahae* mean?

SO HOW DID YOU DO?

0: ARMY card revoked!

1-3: It could be worse, but
are you sure you're ARMY?

4-6: Not bad – but you should
study harder! Still, as Suga always
says, tests aren't everything.

7-9: Pretty good! You're definitely
a big BTS fan, and the boys
would be proud of you.

10: Top of the class! You really
are ARMY – is there anything
you don't know about BTS?

ULTIMATE QUIZ: ANSWERS

1. Bangtan Sonyeondan 2. Jimin and Jungkook 3. *WINGS* 4. Suga, aka Agust D 5. V – he also plays guitar, drums and violin 6. 'DNA', which spent 4 weeks on the chart and peaked at #67 7. RM and J-Hope, who were both born in 1994 8. 'Blood Sweat & Tears' 9. Jin – they even inspired the song 'Tonight' 10. 'I purple you' – which means 'I will trust and love you for a long time', because purple is the last colour of the rainbow.

2021 AND BEYOND

>>>>

In May 2021, BTS's English-language track 'Butter' smashed the charts, immediately hitting #1 on the Billboard Hot 100 and staying there for an incredible 10 weeks. Hot on the heels of their chart-topping success, BTS spoke at the UN General Assembly for a third time about the struggles facing young people during the Covid-19 pandemic. They also performed 'Permission to Dance', joining an elite few artists who have performed at the UN Assembly Hall.

October brought another online concert, watched in nearly 200 countries around the world, before BTS and ARMY were finally reunited in person in November. Across four sold-out nights in LA, BTS performed 'Permission to Dance on Stage' to 214,000 ecstatic fans. Better still, this month brought exciting news that 'Butter' had been nominated for a Grammy.

While the boys weren't able to attend the year-end Korean music awards shows due to Covid-19 restrictions, they swept the board nonetheless, adding plenty of trophies to their bulging cabinets and finishing 2021 on a professional high. And although they didn't win that coveted trophy at the 2022 Grammy Awards, they put on a stunning show, which was the talk of the evening.

So what does the future hold for BTS? Without resident psychic 'Minstradamus' (aka Suga) here to tell us, we'll have to guess. While the Covid-19 pandemic has caused chaos worldwide, BTS will hopefully tour the world and connect with ARMY all across the globe before too long. Undoubtedly there will be new music, more awards and more fun. Watch this space ...